Patricia Kite   *Down in the Sea:*

THE SEA SLUG

Stylocheilus citrina on algae (Hawaii).

ALBERT WHITMAN & COMPANY • Morton Grove, Illinois

To Karen Jeanne Kite—
so lovely, and loves to dance.

Thanks to Terrence M. Gosliner, Ph.D., Senior Curator,
Department of Invertebrate Zoology and Geology,
California Academy of Sciences,
San Francisco, for his help.

Library of Congress Cataloging-in-Publication Data
Kite, L. Patricia.
Down in the sea: The sea slug / Patricia Kite.
p.   cm.
Summary: Describes some of the more than
three thousand types of sea slugs, their habitats,
eating habits, how they reproduce, and how they
protect themselves from enemies.
ISBN 0-8075-1717-8
1. Nudibranchia—Juvenile literature.
[1. Sea slugs.] I. Title.
QL430.4.K57 1994   93-3765
594'.36—dc20   CIP   AC

Cover and interior design:
Karen A. Yops.

The cover shows *Chromodoris willani*
on coral and sponges.

Opposite: *Dirona picta* on red algae (Duxbury Reef, CA).
Above: *Hypselodoris*, species unnamed, on tube coral (Hawaii).

Beautiful sea slugs,
among the most colorful ocean creatures.

Ariolimax columbianus
(banana slug, Washington).

Cepaea nemoralis (land snail)
on beech tree (Germany).

They don't look much like their cousins, land slugs,
or their shell-covered cousins, land and sea snails.

Chromodoris kuniei (Indonesia).

Tridachia crispata (Caribbean).

Hopkinsia rosacea (Duxbury Reef, CA).

Sea slugs can be yellow, purple, green, pink, and many other colors.
They may have spots, stripes, and other decorations.

Flabellina iodinea (California).

Diaulula sandiegensis
in tide pool (Washington).

There are three thousand known types,
and maybe more.
While some are brightly colored,
others are plain.

Hermissenda crassicornis on sponge (British Columbia).

Sea slugs live on sponges, under rocks, on seaweed, in shallow and deep water, in every ocean.

Chromodoris annae on sponge (Indonesia).
This slug is one to three inches long.

Nembrotha kubaryana
(Great Barrier Reef, Australia).
This slug is one to three inches long.

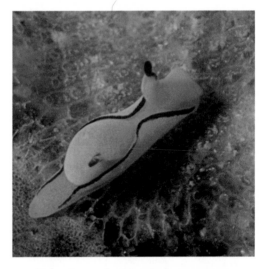

Siphopteron nigromarginatum on sponge
(Papua New Guinea). This slug is
one-quarter inch long.

They can be pinhead size
or as big as watermelons.
Most are in between.

Diver and *Hexabranchus sanguineus* (Indonesia).

Scuba divers see them all the time.

Hornlike bumps

Feelers

Pteraeolidia ianthina (Maui, Hawaii).

Sticking out the front-top of a sea slug's body
are two hornlike bumps.
They act like a nose to sense food.
(Sea slugs don't see well enough to find food.
Their eyes sense only light and dark.)

Hexabranchus sanguineus (Red Sea).

Some sea slugs breathe through their skins.
Others breathe through parts that look
like feathers or fans.

Chromodoris
bullocki
(Fiji).

If pestered, some sea slugs
can swim away,
but not for very long.

Foot

Mostly they crawl, very slowly,
on a single foot made of muscle.
Sea slugs have no bones.

Fryeria, species unnamed, on sponge (Makena, Maui, Hawaii).

Every fish can see bright sea slugs,
and they have no protective shell.
Yet fish don't eat them. Why?
All taste just awful—bitter or mouth-burning.
An enemy does not snack twice.
It sees the bright color
and remembers the awful taste.

Petalifera, species unnamed, on sea grass (Papua New Guinea).

Doto, species unnamed, on hydroid (Papua New Guinea).

Sea slugs protect themselves in other ways, too.
Some look just like their food—
sponges, corals, sea squirts, sea worms.
Can you find the sea slugs in this picture?
An enemy would have trouble finding them, too.

Jason mirabilis (New Zealand).

Phidiana hiltoni (Morro Bay, CA). This slug was just spit out by a fish.
Some back bumps have been nipped; others are completely gone.

If an enemy doesn't leave,
sea slugs with back bumps may bristle them.
This makes them look bigger.
The bumps can break off if an enemy attacks.
The fish will eat the bumps
while the sea slug goes off.
(New back bumps will grow later.)

Glaucus atlanticus feeding on tentacles of *Physalia utriculus*
(Portuguese man-of-war jellyfish) (New South Wales, Australia).

A few sea slugs eat jellyfish,
but jellyfish stingers aren't a bother.
These sea slugs swallow stingers whole
and store them on their back bumps.
If an enemy fish attacks,
the stingers snap out.
The enemy swims off.

Nembrotha lineolata mating (Fiji).

Once a year, or sometimes more,
sea slugs of the same type meet to mate.
Each slug has both male and female body parts,
but needs another slug to fertilize its eggs.

Egg mass

Notodoris, species unnamed, laying eggs (Palau, Micronesia).

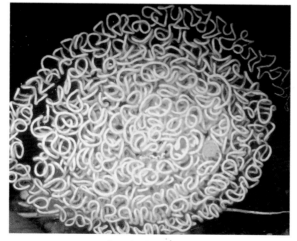

Unidentified egg mass
(Washington).

Berthella martensi egg mass
(Papua New Guinea).

A sea slug can lay one hundred eggs
or up to two million at a time.
The egg groups, curly or ribbony,
are attached to rocks with sticky sea slug mucus.
In two to four weeks they will hatch.
Most of the tiny babies are eaten by fish.
Only one in ten will reach grown-up size.

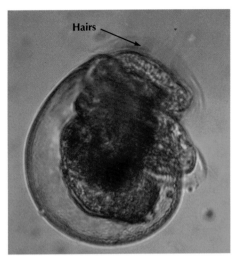

Siphonaria larva, species unnamed (Florida).

Notodoris gardineri adult and young (Coral Sea, Australia).

Baby sea slugs swim very well.
They have shells and look like tiny snails
with hairs sticking out.
The hairs act as paddles and also catch food.
Baby sea slugs need the right food to grow up.
They travel long distances until they sense their meal.
Then they drop down to the food, lose their shells,
and begin to eat and grow.

Phidiana hiltoni in tide pool (Monterey Bay, CA).

Pretty and plain,
sea slugs may live six weeks,
a year, or in between.
Visit a tide pool,
or other quiet ocean place with rocks,
and see how many you can find.

ABOUT SEA SLUGS

Sea slugs belong to the scientific order *Nudibranchia* (pronounced noo-dee-BRANK-ee-a), which means "naked gill." Their ancestors, dating back about 230 million years, had shells. At some point, they began tasting like the bitter food they ate. Enemies did not pursue them, and the shells were no longer needed for protection. Shell-less sea slugs came into being. (Sea slugs are still born with shells, but the shells are left behind when the young slugs leave the *plankton,* a mass of tiny plants and animals that float in the ocean.)

Young sea slugs don't taste bad, so most are eaten. They begin to taste bad after they eat adult food such as sponges and sea anemones.

Camouflage, bristling of back bumps (they are called *cerata* and are special lobes of digestive glands), and the use of jellyfish stingers are some ways sea slugs protect themselves. Additional defenses are an unpleasant smell, poison glands, skin openings that give off sulfuric acid, and bitter mucus secretions. Fish can easily spot the vivid sea slugs, but they remember how bad they tasted. Experiments by Dr. Terrence Gosliner of the California Academy of Sciences have shown that after spitting out a sea slug, a fish will not try to eat one again for a few weeks or even longer.

Sea slugs range in size from a pinhead to a watermelon, but all have within their soft, boneless bodies a heart, a stomach, an anus, a reproductive system, and other complex organs. Each sea slug has both sperm and eggs, but these never mix within a slug. Instead, when sea slugs mate, they fertilize each other's eggs by exchanging sperm.

Sea slugs are seldom seen outside of their natural ocean home. They die rapidly out of water and live only a short time in even the best of aquariums, for the water must be kept at the exact temperature of the sea slug's natural habitat. This is very hard to do. Also, each species is extremely particular about what it will eat. So unless you are a snorkeler or a scuba diver, you will find ocean tide pools to be the best slug theaters.

PHOTO CREDITS: Cover and pp. 4 (bottom), 7, 8 (top), 9: © Dave B. Fleetham/Tom Stack & Associates; pp. 1, 3, 16: © Mike Severns/Tom Stack & Associates; pp. 2, 8 (bottom right), 12 (both), 17 (both), 21 (bottom right), 22 (top): © Terrence M. Gosliner; p. 4 (top left): © Milton Rand/Tom Stack & Associates; p. 4 (top right): Animals, Animals/© 1994, Robert Maier; pp. 5 (top), 13: Animals, Animals/© 1994, W. Gregory Brown; p. 5 (bottom): © Gerald & Buff Corsi/Tom Stack & Associates; p. 6 (left): © Gary Milburn/Tom Stack & Associates; pp. 6 (right), 23: © Jeff Foott/Tom Stack & Associates; p. 8 (bottom left): Animals, Animals/© 1994, Peter Parks, OSF; p. 10: © Ed Robinson/Tom Stack & Associates; pp. 11, 18 (top), 21 (top), 22 (bottom): © Carl Roessler; pp. 14-15, 20: © Mike Bacon/Tom Stack & Associates; p. 18 (bottom): © Ron Russo; p. 19: Animals, Animals/© 1994, Kathie Atkinson, OSF; p. 21 (bottom left): © Evelyn Tronca/Tom Stack & Associates.